# CAMP NOWHERE

## #4 ARE YOU FUR REAL?

BY LEA TADDONIO
ILLUSTRATED BY MICHELLE LAMOREAUX

Spellbound
An Imprint of Magic Wagon
abdopublishing.com

TO JARAH, BRONTE AND POPPY. I LOVE YOU GUYS. - LT

abdopublishing.com

Published by Magic Wagon, a division of ABDO, PO Box 398166,
Minneapolis, Minnesota 55439. Copyright © 2019 by Abdo
Consulting Group, Inc. International copyrights reserved in all
countries. No part of this book may be reproduced in any form
without written permission from the publisher. Spellbound™ is
a trademark and logo of Magic Wagon.

Printed in the United States of America,
North Mankato, Minnesota.
052018
082018

 THIS BOOK CONTAINS
RECYCLED MATERIALS

Written by Lea Taddonio
Illustrated by Michelle Lamoreaux
Edited by Tamara L. Britton
Art Directed by Christina Doffing

Library of Congress Control Number: 2018931958

Publisher's Cataloging-in-Publication Data

Names: Taddonio, Lea, author. | Lamoreaux, Michelle, illustrator.
Title: Are you fur real? / by Lea Taddonio; illustrated by Michelle Lamoreaux.
Description: Minneapolis, Minnesota : Magic Wagon, 2019. |
    Series: Camp nowhere; book 4
Summary: Cooper and Cruz Garcia follow Bigfoot through the woods to his cave.
    They can't believe what they find there! Even more incredible is what they
    learn about Camp Nowhere. Can they keep it a secret?
Identifiers: ISBN 9781532132612 (lib.bdg.) | ISBN 9781532132810 (ebook) |
    ISBN 9781532132919 (Read-to-me ebook)
Subjects: LCSH: Sasquatch--Juvenile fiction. | Siblings--Juvenile fiction. |
    Summer camps-- Juvenile fiction. | Vanishings--Juvenile fiction. |
    Detective and mystery stories--Juvenile fiction.
Classification: DDC [E]--dc23

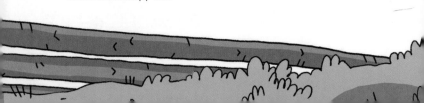

# TABLE OF CONTENTS

# CHAPTER 1
# MY, WHAT BIG FEET

The forest is silent. No birds sing in the trees. All I can hear is my pounding heart.

"Hey. Coop." My brother Cruz pokes my shoulder. "Are you seeing what I'm seeing?"

"That depends." I don't
take my gaze off the monster
blocking our path. "Do you see
Bigfoot?"

"Dude. That thing is either Bigfoot or King Kong's ugly little brother."

The beast has long orange hair and bright red eyes. As for his feet . . . well let's just say "big" doesn't cut it. Hugefoot is a better name.

Bigfoot growls. His voice sounds gravelly, as if it doesn't get much use.

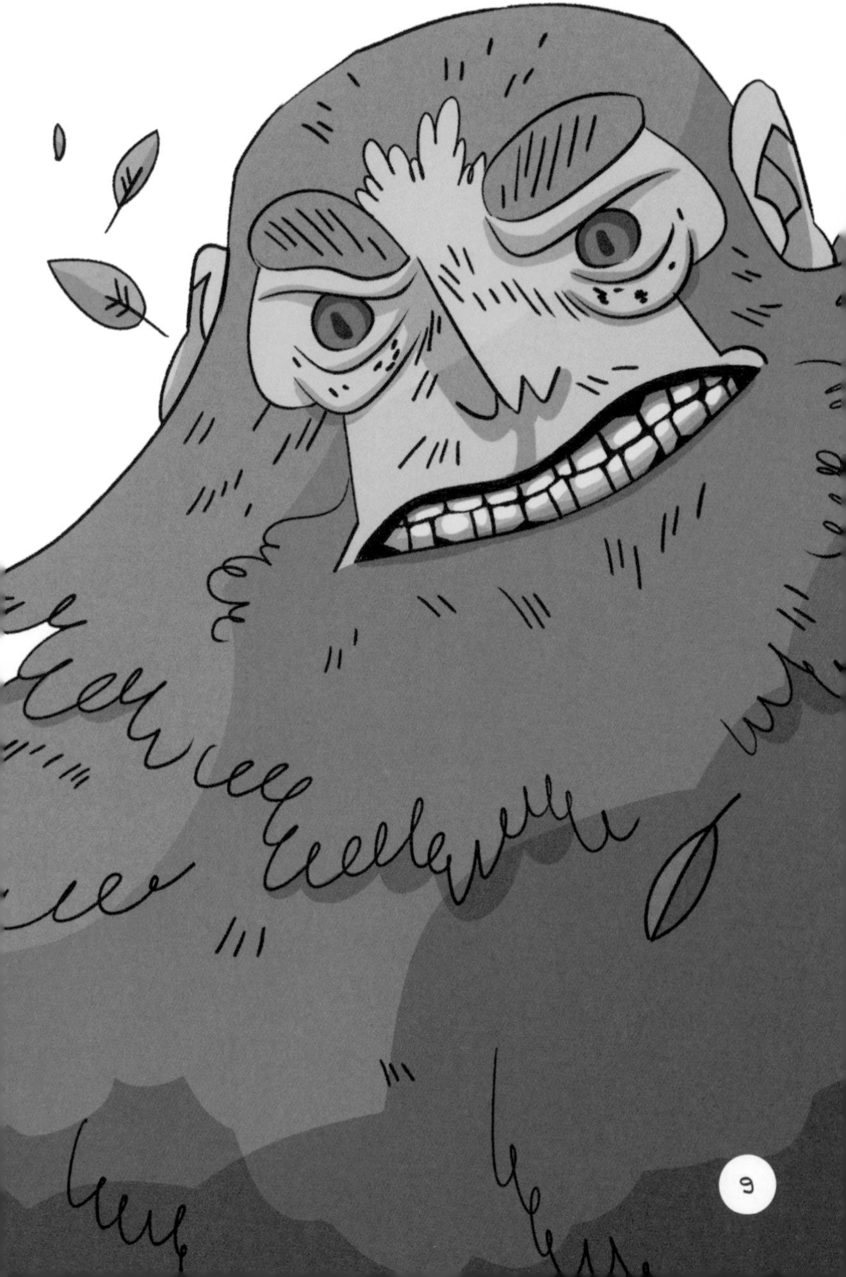

I clear my throat. "Uh. Hi there."

"Are you crazy?" My brother smacks the back of my head. "Be quiet! Don't encourage it."

Before I can yell at my brother for hitting me, Bigfoot steps closer. I can smell his fur. It's a mix between a wet dog and pine trees.

"I'm going to faint or pee my pants," Cruz moans. "Forget it. I'm going to faint AND pee my pants."

I feel the same way. It's hard not to when Bigfoot's mouth is full of sharp teeth.

"G-goodbye w-world," I stammer. I close my eyes. I wait for him to bite off my head.

But nothing happens.

I open one eye. Bigfoot isn't going to eat us. He's pointing up the mountain.

"Do you want us to follow you?" My mouth goes dry. "Have you seen a missing boy? Nick from Woodchuck Cabin?"

But Bigfoot doesn't answer. Instead, he moves into the woods.

Cruz and I look at each other. Should we follow?

# CHAPTER 2
# UP THE MOUNTAIN

Cruz and I decide to trail Bigfoot up the steep mountainside. We don't have a choice. Not if we want to find Nick.

I can't believe this is happening! My brother and I are chasing a Sasquatch. This is a creature that isn't even supposed to exist.

Maybe we will get famous for making a discovery. We could be on television! Or meet the president and get a medal!

Cruz doesn't seem to think
this adventure is as exciting as
I do. In fact, he looks as white as
a ghost.

"How do you know this is safe?" he whispers. "This could be a trap. Watch, it will invite us into its cave and then have us for dinner."

"I think he's friendly." I keep my voice quiet. I don't want to hurt Bigfoot's feelings. He might be scary looking, but he also seems cool.

"Besides," I continue. "This is our chance to help Nick."

"I know." Cruz swipes sweat off his face. "But I don't have to like it."

Bigfoot stops in front of a cave. He points again.

"My bad feelings have bad feelings," Cruz says.

Maybe my brother is right to be worried. Is Bigfoot for real?

## CHAPTER 3
# INTO THE CAVE

"Come on." I grab my brother
by the elbow and step forward.
"Nick could be hurt ... or
worse!"

We enter the cave. It's cozy and snug. Dried leaves are piled up to make a bed in one corner.

Next to a small fire is Nick.

He's fast asleep but alive.

Bigfoot looks at our
cabinmate's ankle. It's puffy,
purple, and angry looking.

"Cooper? Cruz?" Nick stirs awake. "What are you guys doing here?"

"We came looking for you," I say. "You're missing. Everyone at Camp Nowhere is worried!"

"We thought he took you!" Cruz pointed to Bigfoot.

Nick laughs before gasping in pain. "Ooof, it hurts to do that. No! I fell while running away and twisted my ankle on a stupid log."

"You were running away from Camp Nowhere?" I ask.

"I wanted to go home," Nick says. "But I got lost in the woods and this big guy rescued me." He lifts his hand and Bigfoot fist bumps him.

"He's really friendly," Nick continues. "He picked me berries to eat and built me this fire."

Before we can ask any
more questions, Bigfoot turns
quickly toward the cave
entrance.

Someone is coming.

# CHAPTER 4

# THE SECRET

"What's up, Biggie?"
Counselor Bob ducks into the
cave. He trails off when he
notices Cruz and I standing
there. "Cooper! Cruz! What are
you two doing here?"

"We wanted to find Nick,"
I say. "We found a tear in
our window screen and a big
footprint behind the cabin."

"We thought that Bigfoot took him!" Cruz said.

"Biggie!" Counselor Bob cries. "You have to stop stealing cookies and candy from the campers' cabins."

"Biggie wouldn't hurt a fly," Counselor Bobs says. "In fact, he finds all of our camp runaways."

"You mean those missing kids from last year?" I ask.

"Exactly. But people can't know there is a Sasquatch here. No one will come to Camp Nowhere anymore! So you will have to be sent home like they were. Before you can tell the other campers."

"Sent home?" This is what we had wanted. Why don't I feel happy? Cruz doesn't look too excited either.

"I'm sorry I tried to run away," Nick says. "It was a mistake. I want to give camp a second chance."

"What if we promise never to tell anyone?" Cruz asks. "Could we stay then?"

"You can keep a secret?" Counselor Bob looks around at all of us.

We nod. And we do.

For the rest of summer we never speak a word about Bigfoot. We tell everyone at camp we were lost in the woods and rescued by Counselor Bob.

But every week we sneak up to Bigfoot's cave and bring him cookies and candy.

It turns out the best part of summer camp are the friends you make.